· A COAT FOR THE MOON AND OTHER JEWISH TALES ·

A Coat for the Moon
and
other Jewish Tales

SELECTED AND RETOLD BY
Howard Schwartz AND Barbara Rush

ILLUSTRATED BY
Michael Iofin

THE JEWISH PUBLICATION SOCIETY

PHILADELPHIA

1999 • 5759

The Jewish Publication Society
2100 Arch Street, 2nd Floor
Philadelphia, PA 19103-1399

"The Rusty Plate" previously appeared in *Spider*. "The Weaving that Saved the Prince" previously appeared in *Cricket*. "The Queen of the Sea" and "A Family of Demons" previously appeared in *The Sagarin Review*.

Design by Nachman Elsner
Composition by Elsner Design
Manufactured in the United States of America

The Library of Congress has cataloged the hardcover edition of this title as:
Schwartz, Howard, 1945-
     A coat for the moon and other Jewish Tales / Selected & retold by
Howard Schwartz and Barabara Rush: illustrated by Michael Iofin.
     p.   cm.
Summary: A collection of Jewish folktales from around the world, including "The lamp on the Mountain," "The Witch Barusha," "The Sabbath Walking Stick," and "The Fisherman and the Silver Fish."
ISBN 0-8276-0596-X (alk. paper)–cloth
ISBN 0-8276-0736-9–paper
1. Jews–Folklore. 2. Tales. [1. Jews–Folklore. 2. Folklore.]
I. Rush, Barbara. II. Iofin, Michael, ill. III. Title.
PZB.1.S4Co 1999
398.2'089924–dc21   98-52704
                                                                          CIP
                                                                          AC

05 04 03 02   5 4 3

For Shira, Nathan, and Miriam
— H.S.

In memory of Matan,
my young grandson,
and in celebration of Ilan,
my newest grandchild
— B.R.

· CONTENTS ·

· INTRODUCTION ·

In the game of "Telephone", a group of children sit in a circle and one whispers a secret to the next. The secret is repeated until the last child to hear it tells the others what he or she heard, and it is almost always different from what was told at first. Folklore—especially Jewish folklore—is a lot like this game, but instead of being played in one time and place, it is played all over the world and takes place over many centuries.

The Jews are a wandering people, and they often bring the stories they have heard in their travels from one country to the next. In this way, these stories changed, and many versions of them came to be scattered all over the world.

In this book we have gathered some of the best tales that have been told to Jewish children over the centuries, from Eastern Europe to the Middle East. The children's parents or grandparents usually told them these stories at night, before they went to sleep. Many are stories about Jewish heroes, such as King David or King Solomon, but more often they are stories about poor people, like the parents who told them and the children who listened.

At the same time, many of these tales are filled with magic. In France they tell of an enchanted spring whose waters let whoever drinks from it understand the language of the birds. In Turkey they tell of a Sabbath walking stick that brings a wonderful Sabbath meal to the poorest Jew. And in Morocco they tell of an ancient silver fish from the time of Moses that can grant magic wishes to whoever catches it and lets it go.

Some of these stories are also scary. In Yemen the people worried that the witch Barusha would slip into their houses and turn their newborn babies into puppies. And they sometimes tell us of strange worlds, like the underground world of Tevel, in which people have two heads. And sometimes these tales are simply fun or even silly, like the story of the tailors who wanted to sew a coat for the moon.

But in all these stories, God watches over the Jews and protects them in wonderful ways. Sometimes God sends the prophet Elijah to help those in need, or sometimes help comes from a rabbi whose faith is strong enough to overcome the forces of evil.

These stories are a gateway to our past. Hidden in these stories are the lives of our ancestors. What can we learn about them from these tales? We can see that their lives were hard, that they were often hungry or afraid. And, to reassure themselves, they told these old stories, which gave them courage in times of danger.

When you read these stories, try to imagine the faces of those who told them, for those are the faces of your own ancestors. And once you have read them, remember to share them with someone else, so that the game of telephone, which started so many centuries ago, can continue in your own generation.

YOU WILL COME BACK HERE." THE QUEEN DIDN'T WANT DANIEL TO LEAVE, BUT SHE DIDN'T WANT HIM TO BE UNHAPPY EITHER. "VERY WELL," SHE SAID, "YOU MAY RETURN TO YOUR FORMER HOME, BUT YOU MUST PROMISE THAT ONCE A YEAR, ON THIS VERY DAY, YOU WILL COME BACK HERE."

· THE QUEEN OF THE SEA ·

Long ago, in the land of Egypt, there was a young boy named Daniel who lived near the sea. He loved to swim in the waves and to bask in the sun. One day, as he was walking on the beach, he saw a small turtle in the sand, its foot stuck beneath a rock. The poor animal was so hot, so dry from being in the sun, that it could hardly move. "Oh, you poor turtle," said the boy, "you will surely die if I don't set you free." And so he picked up the turtle and returned it to the water.

Now, if the truth be known, that was the pet turtle of the Queen of the Sea, who lived in an underwater palace from which she ruled all the creatures of the ocean. She was delighted to see her turtle again, for she had feared that it was lost, and she was pleased to learn about the boy who had rescued it.

Years passed. The boy grew into a young man. He married and built a fine house near the sea. But one day, as he was swimming in the water, a storm suddenly arose, and a huge whirlpool dragged him beneath the waves.

As Daniel sank into the sea, a giant turtle suddenly appeared. It was the very same turtle he had saved many years before, now grown to one hundred times its original size. The turtle carried Daniel on its back through the water and, strange as it may seem, Daniel had no trouble breathing at all.

Soon Daniel and the turtle reached the palace of the Queen of the Sea. She sat on a high throne, dressed in a gown of purple seaweed, with a crown of pearls and coral on her head. She was very beautiful, and the pearl in the center of her crown glowed with a light of its own.

"Welcome, Daniel," said the queen kindly. "I saw in my magic mirror that you were drowning. It is I who sent the turtle to save you. This is your reward for helping it so long ago."

Daniel was amazed. "Where am I? And how can I breathe under water?" he asked.

"Ah, that is part of my enchantment," replied the queen. "Come, I will show you." And as she led the young man through the rooms of her palace, he saw that it was more magnificent than anything he could have imagined.

The queen invited Daniel to remain with her in that underwater palace, and so he did. His days were filled with happiness as he and the queen swam in the clear waters, surrounded by fish of every color of the rainbow. Playful starfish and curly sea horses bobbed up and down around them. And the queen taught Daniel the language of every creature that lived in the sea. Soon he came to understand the squealing of dolphins, the barking of seals, and the singing of whales.

Daniel was so enchanted by the powers of the queen that he forgot his wife and his friends. The queen, indeed, wanted him to remain there forever, and Daniel knew that even if he asked to leave, she would not let him go. So it was that he lived in the palace for many years.

But there came a time when he longed so much for his earthly home that he grew very sad. The queen asked, "Daniel, what troubles you? Perhaps I can help."

"Indeed," he answered, "I long to see my wife again, and to walk in the warm sand, and to feel the sun once more on my face."

The queen didn't want Daniel to leave, but she didn't want him to be unhappy either. "Very well," she said, "you may return to your former home, but you must promise that once a year, on this very day, you will return to visit me. The turtle will be waiting to bring you back. And you must never tell anyone where you have been, for if you do, you will regret it."

"I promise to do as you say," Daniel replied.

"Then you may take your leave," the queen said, and she commanded the giant turtle to take Daniel back to the shore of his land. At last he was returning to his home.

You can imagine how surprised and overjoyed his wife was to see him! Why, she had been sure that he had drowned and that she would never see him again. And she began to ask, "Daniel, where have you been? How could you have remained alive?"

Daniel knew that he had to tell her something, but he did not dare tell the truth. So he said that he had been carried off by a great wave and stranded on a desert island until a passing ship had found him and brought him back.

Now, Daniel did not forget his promise to the queen. The next year, on the very day that he had returned from the underwater palace, Daniel disappeared. And when he returned the next day, his wife asked, "Daniel, where have you been?" This time Daniel gave no answer, and she began to weep and cry aloud.

A year later, after Daniel had once again disappeared for a day, his wife asked, "Daniel, tell me, where do you go when you disappear once a year?" But, once again, Daniel gave no answer. After that she began to torment him: "Oh, my husband, you never tell me anything! You are keeping secrets from me!"

And then, one year after that, when Daniel disappeared for a third time, his wife pretended to be ill. "Daniel," she sighed, "where is it that you go every year? I will surely die if I don't learn the secret."

Afraid that his wife was really very sick, Daniel began to tell her the story. "You see, there was a giant turtle that took me to a palace beneath the sea. . . ." But the secret had no sooner left his lips than a fierce wind blew up from the sea, dashed in through the window, and carried Daniel away. Soon he was being whirled around and around in the air, until the whirlwind descended into the sea, forming a whirlpool, and Daniel was pulled inside the underwater palace.

Instantly the queen appeared, and Daniel could see that she was furious. "So, you broke your promise, did you?" she shrieked. And before Daniel could even reply, the queen ordered her guards to imprison him.

Frightened beyond words, Daniel began to stammer. "P-p-please, is there no way I can redeem myself? Is there nothing I can do?"

The queen scowled. But then she thought of a plan. "Yes," she said, "there is one thing. A few days ago the glowing pearl in my crown, the only one of its kind, was stolen, and, despite all my powers, I have not been able to find the thief. I will give you three days to search for it. If you can find my pearl, you will be forgiven, but if you do not, you will return to prison."

So Daniel journeyed to all parts of the sea, to where the waters were warm as well as to where they were cold. For two days he could find no trace of the missing pearl. But on the third day he heard two mermaids speaking in an underwater cave, and he listened to everything they said.

"The queen is angry," said one, "because her precious pearl is missing."

"We are lucky she doesn't know we are the thieves!" said the other, "for in these dark waters nothing is more precious than that glowing pearl." Now, the mermaids spoke in their own language, which no human could ever understand. But since Daniel knew the language of every sea creature, he understood their words as well. He followed the mermaids a great distance to the place where they had hidden the pearl. As they lifted a rock, the light of the pearl shone forth. And when they saw that it was still there, the mermaids swam away.

As soon as they were gone, Daniel lifted the rock and recovered the glowing pearl. He took it back to the queen at once. She was so happy that she forgave Daniel and freed him from his vow forever, and, as a reward, she gave him a golden box filled with pearls. Then she called her giant turtle to take him back to his home, and before long Daniel stood on the shore again, far from the palace beneath the sea.

Daniel's wife was so glad to see him that she never again nagged him to try to learn his secrets. As for Daniel, he had learned a lesson, and never again did he break a promise.

Every year, on the day when he used to go to the Queen of the Sea, Daniel sold one of the pearls, and, with the money he received, he and his wife were able to live in comfort and to share their wealth with those in need. When Daniel and his wife had children, they told them this story and showed them the box of pearls. And they all lived in happiness and great wealth.

Egypt: Oral Tradition

"...WITH THOSE WHO HAVE LESS THAN I DO." "BECAUSE YOU GAVE ME ONE PIECE OF BREAD," DAVID TOLD HIM, "YOUR LIFE WAS SAVED." "YOU CAN BE SURE," THE MAN SAID, "THAT FROM NOW ON I WILL SHARE WHATEVER I HAVE WITH THOSE WHO HAVE LESS THAN I DO."

· THE ENCHANTED SPRING ·

When King David was a boy, he loved to roam in the forest. There he watched birds building nests, squirrels jumping from tree to tree, and snails slipping through the grass.

Sometimes he would play beautiful songs on his harp, but at other times he would make no sound at all so he could hear the music of the forest—the songs of birds and insects and the sound of wind rustling through the leaves.

One day, when David had walked farther into the forest than he had ever gone before, he heard the sound of bubbling water. Was there a spring nearby? David was very tired and thirsty, so he pushed through a tangle of bushes and vines, and, much to his delight, he found a little spring bubbling up at the base of a tree.

The water was unusually pure and clear, so David bent over and sipped some of it from his cupped hands. Suddenly he no longer felt tired, and, even more mysterious, he began to hear voices coming from the trees.

At first David thought that someone else was near him in the forest. Then he realized he had overheard two birds chirping to each other. The chirps had sounded like words! That is how David came to understand that the waters of the spring were enchanted.

As David returned home, he passed many birds and animals, and, to his amazement, he understood every chirp and snort and growl. He heard a bird saying, "God plans to punish a rich but stingy man by sending a poisonous snake to his house."

"Do you mean the man who buried a chest full of silver and gold under the oak tree near his front door?" a second bird asked.

"Yes," said the first, "that man never gives charity to anyone. He even sends beggars away empty-handed."

"But it would be sad if the snake killed him," said the second bird. "It's a pity he doesn't know that he can avoid the danger if he keeps the snake out of his house all night, since the snake will lose its power at dawn."

"That is true," answered the first bird, "but few are wise enough to escape."

David knew at once who the man was, for he was well-known for his stinginess. And when David heard what the birds said, he hurried to the rich man's house to warn him.

When David got there, he looked through the window and saw that the man was eating dinner with his wife and son and daughter.

"I will see if this man is as stingy as everyone says," David thought to himself. So he knocked on the door.

"Who's there?" asked the rich man.

"A beggar boy," David answered. "I am very hungry. Please give me something to eat."

"Go away," said the rich man. "I don't give food to beggars."

But the man's son said, "Daddy, look, we have extra bread on our plates. Let's give some to the hungry boy."

"No, let him go hungry," said the man.

"Please, Daddy," begged the daughter. "The boy sounds so sad. Give him one piece of bread."

Finally the rich man agreed. "Very well," he called. "We will give you some bread, but be on your way at once."

When the man opened the door, David hurried inside. "Quick," he said. "A poisonous snake is on its way here to bite you. Do as I say if you want to be saved."

The man was astonished. "How can I believe such a thing?" he asked.

"Are you the man who buried a chest full of silver and gold under your oak tree?" David asked. "If so, you are the man the snake is coming to bite."

The rich man turned white with fear. He knew that David must be speaking the truth, for he had never told anyone about the treasure he had hidden under the tree.

"What must I do?" he gasped.

"If you can keep the snake away until dawn, you will be saved," David told him. "But take no chances with your family. Send them away. Only you and I will stay here. And hurry, for the snake will arrive by nightfall."

The man sent his wife and his daughter and his son into the woods, each in a different direction. Then he locked the door with seven locks.

The moment he finished locking the seventh lock, he and David heard someone knocking.

"Who is it?" the man called.

A voice replied, "It is your wife. Please open the door. It's cold outside. Let me in."

The voice was the voice of his beloved wife, and the man wanted to let her in. But David held him back. "No," he shouted, "it's not your wife—it's the snake. Listen closely and you will hear it hissing."

The voice at the door continued to plead, "Please, let me in, let me in." But the man listened, and he heard the hiss. And he did not open the door.

An hour later there was another knock at the door. A voice spoke. This time it sounded like the man's son. "Daddy, Daddy, open the door. There are wolves outside, and I am afraid. Please let me in." The man jumped up to open the door for his beloved son.

But David held him back. "That is not your son. It is the snake again. Listen carefully." The man listened and again he heard the hissing. And he did not open the door.

All night long, David and the man waited. Just before dawn there was another knocking at the door. This time the man heard the voice of his daughter. "Daddy, Daddy, it's dark outside, and I'm afraid. Please, hurry and let me in." Now the man rushed to open the door for his beloved daughter. But David held him back and told him it was the snake. The man listened and heard the hissing. And he did not open the door.

Soon the first light of day appeared in the sky. "We have won!" David cried, hugging the man. "You have escaped the poisonous snake!"

The man opened the door and rushed outside to look for his wife and son and daughter. They were coming down the road, safe and very happy to see him. The family kissed and hugged each other and then kissed and hugged David as well. The man thanked David with all his heart for saving him.

"Because you gave me one piece of bread," David told him, "your life was saved."

"You can be sure," the man said, "that from now on I will share whatever I have with those who have less than I do."

And so he did. After that, no beggar ever left his door without a fine meal. And the rich man always told them the story of how the boy David had saved his life.

As for David, he returned to the forest from time to time and drank from the waters of the enchanted spring. Then he would listen to the talk of the birds. If there were people in need, he would do his best to help them, just as he had helped the stingy man. And when he grew up, David continued to go to that spring, and the wisdom he gained there helped him become a great king whose deeds are remembered even to this day.

France: Thirteenth Century

· THE LAMP ON THE MOUNTAIN ·

Long ago, in the days of King David, there lived a man who was very poor. All week long he worked hard, yet, when Friday came, he and his wife did not have enough money to bake a *challah* or to buy candles and wine for their table. So he went to a rich man to ask for help.

"Yes, I will give you money for the Sabbath and a big bag of gold besides," answered the rich man, "but only if you fulfill this task. On the highest mountain near our village, it is very cold. If you can remain naked all night on top of that mountain, the money will be yours."

The poor man was embarrassed. He did not want to go. But he needed the money for the Sabbath, so he agreed. That night he climbed to the top of the mountain, took off his clothes and tried to go to sleep. But it was freezing there on that mountain top, and his teeth chattered, and his fingers turned blue. He did not get a single moment's sleep. But as cold as he was, he was determined to remain there all night, and so he did.

In the morning the poor man climbed down the mountain, got dressed, and ran to the rich man's house. "I did as you asked and spent the night naked on top of the mountain. Now I have come to claim the money you promised," he cried.

"Oh, but I will not pay you the money," said the rich man, "for you did not win it in a fair way. On the top of a nearby mountain is a lamp that burns day and night. Surely the light from that lamp kept you warm, and only because of that lamp were you able to stay on the mountain all night long."

"You are the one who is not fair," cried the poor man. "I stayed on top of that cold mountain all night long, but now you refuse to pay me. Let us go to King David and ask him to decide who is right."

And so the two men went to the palace of the king. That day the king's young son, Solomon, was seated near his father's throne, and when the two men approached, King David bent down and said, "Today, Solomon, you may help me make a decision."

So both King David and young Solomon listened to the arguments of the two men.

"This rich man promised me money if I remained naked on top of the cold mountain all night long, which I did," said the poor man.

"But he was really warmed by the light of a lamp from a nearby mountain," protested the rich man.

King David listened. He hesitated. He did not know what to answer. Then the boy, Solomon, spoke up. "Father," he said, "it is difficult to decide while we are so hungry. Let us have a lunch of fine roast lamb and invite these two men to join us. Then, after lunch, you can make your decision."

The king agreed. Everyone sat down at a fine table. Nearby a platter was heaped with large pieces of cold, raw lamb. Solomon asked the servants to light the cooking fire in the next room. They all waited: King David, young Solomon, the poor man, and the rich man. How hungry they were!

Ten minutes!

Twenty minutes!

Thirty minutes went by!

Then Solomon spoke. "The lamb is roasted. Now we may eat!" The servants sliced a piece of lamb for each guest and put it on a plate.

But when the rich man saw his piece, he cried aloud, "How can I eat this meat? It is raw!"

"What do you mean?" answered Solomon. "The meat is done. It was cooked by the fire in the next room."

"But, my dear prince," said the rich man, "how can a fire in a nearby room cook the meat in this room? The fire is too far away."

Solomon replied, "If you can believe that a lamp from a nearby mountain could warm the body of this man, then surely you can see that the fire from a nearby room could roast this meat."

When King David heard those words, he knew what decision to make.

At once he ordered the rich man to give the poor man the money that he had promised him. And so the man did.

That Friday night, the poor family had a fine Sabbath meal. As for the rich man, he never tried to fool anyone again. And young Solomon grew up to become a king who was a wise and clever judge.

Turkey: Oral Tradition

"...AND THEY BEGIN TO FIGHT"..."YOU HAVE NO IDEA WHAT IT'S LIKE TO LIVE IN A LAND WHERE EVERYONE HAS TWO HEADS; THERE IS NO PEACE. WHENEVER SOMEONE'S HEAD SAYS, 'LET'S GO IN THIS DIRECTION,' THE OTHER ANSWERS, 'NO, LET'S GO THE OTHER WAY,'

· THE UNDERGROUND WORLD ·

King Solomon had traveled to every place on the face of the earth. One day he was boasting to his most trusted advisor, Bennyahu: "My magic carpet has taken me across the greatest oceans, to the tops of the highest mountains, and through the driest deserts. Yes, my dear Bennyahu, there is no place in the world that I have not seen."

At that moment, the king heard a strange voice, and a visitor appeared from nowhere and stood before the king. "But Solomon," the voice said, "have you been to the land that is underground?"

Solomon knew the visitor at once; it was none other than Ashmodai, King of the Demons. Many years before, Solomon had captured Ashmodai, who later had tricked the king into giving up his magic ring. And before Solomon had been able to get it back, he had been forced to wander as a beggar for many years while Ashmodai ruled in his place. Now the King of Demons could not bear to hear Solomon's boasting. "Have you been to the underground world?" he asked again.

"Underground?" the king wondered. "Bennyahu, you have traveled to all corners of the earth to do my bidding. Have you ever seen such a place?"

"My king, I did hear talk of such a place, but in all my travels I have never come across it."

So King Solomon laughed at the demon king, "An underground world? A ridiculous notion! If there is such a place, prove it to me. Bring me one of its inhabitants!"

Ashmodai answered, "Indeed, Solomon, if it's proof you want, just watch!"

Then the demon king reached his hand into the ground and stretched and stretched and stretched until his hand reached a place in the depths of the earth, and from that place he pulled forth a creature that seemed human in every way except that it had two heads and four eyes.

Solomon gasped in amazement. "I never thought such a being could exist," he cried. "This is truly astonishing." The demon king said "There is nothing new on the face of the earth, but this man has never been seen on the face of the earth. He is from Tevel." Then Ashmodai bowed and took his leave, while the two-headed man stayed behind. When the creature saw that he had not been forced to return to the world underground, he sighed with relief and said, "Oh, thank God I am out of that place!"

"And what place is that?" asked Solomon in amazement. "Who are you and where do you come from?"

"I am a descendant of Cain, and I come from a land called Tevel that is far beneath the earth."

"And what kind of place is it? Do you have a sun and a moon in your land?" asked Bennyahu, who was as astonished as the king.

"Yes, and we farm and plow just as you do."

"And do you pray?" asked the king.

"Oh, yes," replied the man from Tevel. "We thank the Lord for creating us and all other living creatures. And I thank you, as well, for setting me free from that awful place."

Solomon was puzzled. "And why is that?" he asked.

"Ah," replied the creature, with a greater sigh than before, "you have no idea what it's like to live in a land where everyone has two heads. There is no peace. Whenever someone's head says, 'Let's go in this direction,' the other answers, 'No, let's go the other way.' And they begin to argue. When the two heads are finished with a meal, one head yells, 'You ate more than I did.' 'No,' cries the second, 'you ate more!' All day long there is so much noise I can hardly bear it." And the creature's second head nodded in agreement.

Then the creature fell before the king and begged not to be sent back to his underground home.

King Solomon agreed to let the strange visitor from Tevel remain in his kingdom, and even saw to it that he was married to a human wife. The husband worked hard farming the land, and he became very rich. In time the couple had six sons who resembled their mother and had only one head, and a seventh son who had two heads like his father.

At last the man from Tevel grew old and died, and the son who resembled him demanded two portions of his inheritance. "After all," he said, "I have twice as many heads as my brothers, so it is only fair that I receive twice as much as they." But his brothers disagreed. "You have only one body," they argued. "Therefore, you should receive only one portion." The sons continued to argue and could not come to an agreement. And so, at last, they went to King Solomon to ask him to decide the matter.

King Solomon asked for boiling water to be brought to him. He then commanded one of his servants to pour the hot water over one of the man's heads, but just as the servant was about to do so, both heads began to scream at the same time, "No, no, don't burn me!" King Solomon stopped the servant with his outstretched hand and said, "You see, both heads are afraid. That proves that they are one."

So it was that the two-headed son received only a single portion of his father's inheritance, and never again did he claim that he deserved twice as much as anyone else. So too did King Solomon continue to reign over his people and to judge them wisely for many years.

Ancient Israel: circa Fifth Century

· THE DEMON IN THE WINE CELLAR ·

King Solomon was a very wise king who knew the ways of magic. It happened one day that some of his best bottles of wine turned to vinegar. Solomon sent his servant back to the wine cellar four times before he found a bottle of wine that was not spoiled. The king began to suspect that a demon was playing tricks on him, and he decided to find out.

Solomon had the floor of the wine cellar covered with ashes, and the next morning when he went to inspect it, he found footprints like those of a rooster. "Just as I thought," said the king, "these footprints were made by a demon!" For King Solomon had seen the footprints of a demon before. And he knew that he had to get rid of it.

The first thing King Solomon did was to hide a guard inside one of the barrels in the wine cellar. The guard kept watch through a hole in the barrel, and at midnight he saw the demon arrive and take one of the most valuable bottles of the king's wine. The demon pulled out the cork and drank till the bottle was empty. Then it poured some vinegar into the bottle, replaced the cork, and put the bottle back in place. After that, the demon disappeared.

The next morning, the guard told the king all that he had seen, and Solomon thought of a plan. He ordered sleeping powder to be put into six of the most precious bottles in the wine cellar, and he told the guard to hide in the barrel for another night. At exactly midnight, the demon appeared out of nowhere and went right to the best bottles of wine, pulling out one of the six bottles with the sleeping powder. The demon drank the whole bottle in one swallow, and all of a sudden began to stagger about. A minute later the demon was snoring loudly.

Now, as soon as this happened, the guard climbed out of the barrel, tied the demon with a chain, and went off to call the king. King Solomon hurried to the wine cellar, arriving just as the demon was opening its eyes.

"Well, demon," said the king, "did you enjoy my wine? I hope you will enjoy my winepress as well—for I plan to put you through it!"

"No! No!" cried the demon, "anything but that! I'll do whatever you want! Please, spare me!"

The king thought for a moment, and then he said, "Well, there is one way that you could save yourself. I've heard it said that demons can turn themselves into smoke and enter empty bottles. But I don't suppose that you could…"

And before King Solomon could finish his words—Poof! The demon turned itself into a puff of smoke and swirled down into an empty bottle. That was the moment the king had been waiting for. As quickly as he could, he sealed the bottle with a cork and said to the guard, "Take this bottle out to the middle of the sea and cast it into the water."

And that is exactly what the guard did. So it was that the bottle sank to the bottom of the ocean, where it remained for a long, long time. Thus did King Solomon rid himself of that demon.

Many years later, a current picked up that bottle and carried it close to shore. One day a poor man walking along a beach saw the bottle floating nearby. The man, being curious, waded into the water to get it. Now, the bottle was quite heavy, but this made the man even more curious. "Surely there is something good inside it!" he thought.

But when the man pulled out the cork, what did he see rising from the bottle but a great pillar of smoke that slowly took the shape of a giant demon! The poor man was speechless.

In an instant, the demon stood before him. "Free at last!" it shouted.

"G-g-good morning," stammered the poor man.

"I have been locked up inside that bottle for hundreds of years," said the demon, "since the days of King Solomon. I am very hungry and thirsty. Give me something to eat and something to drink."

"Alas, I have nothing to offer you," answered the poor man. "That is why I was walking on the beach—I too was looking for something to eat."

"Look," shrieked the demon, "you are the one who took me out of the bottle, and you are responsible for feeding me!"

"What can I do?" asked the poor man. "I am as hungry and thirsty as you are."

"Listen," the demon threatened, "give me something to eat or I will eat you!"

"Please, please, please," begged the poor man, "let me go. If I had anything to give you, I would."

"In that case," said the demon, "let a judge decide between us."

So the demon and the man appeared before a judge. "This man has pulled me out of a bottle," the demon said, "but now he refuses to feed me."

"But I have no food to give it," protested the man.

The judge thought for a moment. Then he said, "The demon is right. The man must either return the demon to the bottle or feed it!"

Now, because the poor man had no way to do either, the two agreed to go to another judge—and still another. And each judge said the same thing: "The man must either return the demon to the bottle or feed it!"

The man was truly frightened, for he was sure that the demon would devour him. He ran from the demon as fast as he could. The demon, of course, ran after him, and soon the two came to a forest where they saw a fox. The demon wanted to eat it too, and the fox was forced to leap up onto a high rock to escape. From there it called, "Demon, why are you chasing this man?"

"This man has pulled me out of a bottle, and now he refuses to feed me," explained the demon.

"Is this true?" asked the fox.

"Yes," said the man, "when I uncorked the bottle, the demon came out in a great puff of smoke, but I have no food to give it."

"You are both liars!" cried the fox. "How can a demon turn into smoke? Only if I saw it with my own eyes would I believe such foolishness!"

"What? Are you calling me a liar?" shrieked the demon. "I will show you that I am speaking the truth." And to prove it, the demon began to turn itself back into smoke.

"Are you satisfied now?" it called as it slowly disappeared.

"That is not enough!" cried the fox. "I won't believe it unless I see you enter the bottle."

So the demon, now mostly made of smoke, entered the bottle, except for its head. "There, are you satisfied now?" it shouted.

"No," said the fox, "I won't believe it until I see your head in the bottle as well."

"Then watch carefully," called the demon, and—Poof!—it turned completely to smoke and sank into the bottle.

"Quick! This is your chance," the fox shouted to the man. "Seal the bottle and throw it into the sea!"

The fox did not have to tell the poor man twice! He quickly pushed the cork in as far as it would go, rushed to the sea, and threw the demon back into the water, where it sank into the depths. And, for all we know, the bottle—and the demon—are still there.

Yemen: Oral Tradition

COLORS OF THE RAINBOW. AT THE VERY MOMENT THEY THE POOR JEW UNWRAPPED HIS RUSTY PLATE, ELIJAH PUSHED THE PLATE UNDER THE WINDOW, SO THAT THE SUN SHONE UPON IT, AND WITHIN A MOMENT THE PLATE GLISTENED AND SPARKLED WITH ALL THE

· THE RUSTY PLATE ·

The king was having a birthday, and his subjects all wanted to give him a present. Some sent jewels for his crown, some sent bags of gold and silver, and some sent fine cloth and embroideries. Every day hundreds of people stood in line outside the palace, waiting to present their birthday gifts to the king.

In a small village far from the capital city, there lived a Jew who was too poor to buy a gift. But he wanted so much to give the king a present! He looked all over his house: in the closets, in the kitchen, and even under the bed. But he found nothing fit for a king.

Now, this poor Jew had a neighbor who was rich. And when the neighbor saw the Jew searching everywhere, he scoffed, "What could you possibly have that would be worthy of a king?"

The very next day, the rich neighbor found a broken, rusty plate lying in the poor man's yard. "Why don't you take this old plate to the palace?" he cried in a mocking tone. "Surely it will make a perfect present for the king!"

When the poor Jew heard these words, his heart was filled with joy. "Yes," he repeated, "this will make a perfect present for the king. Why didn't I think of it myself? I will go at once."

And so the poor man wrapped the plate in a piece of clean cloth and walked to the capital city, so far away. As he walked along, his heart was happy. "I am bringing the king a special gift," he thought. "I am bringing him something from my own yard. Surely the King will be pleased."

When at last he reached the palace, the poor Jew stood in the long line of people waiting to present their gifts. When he finally stood before the king himself, the Jew unwrapped his rusty plate and placed it at the king's feet.

At that very moment God looked down and saw the deed of the poor Jew. God saw how kind the man's heart was, and how much he wanted to please the king. And God smiled. Then God sent Elijah the Prophet down to the palace disguised as a helper to the king.

When the poor Jew unwrapped his rusty plate, Elijah pushed it under the window so that the sun shone upon it. The plate glistened and sparkled with all the colors of the rainbow. Then Elijah turned the plate from side to side, and the rusty spots shone like precious diamonds.

The king was amazed. "Never have I seen such a beautiful plate!" he cried, jumping to his feet. The king ordered Elijah to put it on a special shelf near the window so that he could gaze upon it. "How can I thank you, my dear man?" the king asked the poor Jew. "I know! I will give you a gift in return." And the king bade the Jew wait outside. In a short while the king's servants brought him a pouch with his gift inside.

The poor Jew set out for his village, delighted that his present had found favor with the king. When he reached home, he opened the pouch and, to his great surprise, found that it was filled with gold coins.

The next day the rich neighbor saw the bag of gold, and he was curious about it. "Where did you get so much gold?" he asked. The poor Jew told him what had happened at the palace.

"Ah," thought the rich neighbor, "if the king gave *him* a bag of gold for his old, rusty plate, imagine what he would give *me* for a plate of real gold!" So the man sold all his jewels, all his embroideries, all his precious possessions, and had a plate made of solid gold.

He wrapped it in silk and rode to the capital city. He, too, waited in line, and when at last it was his turn to stand before the king, he unwrapped his gift and placed it at the king's feet.

The plate sparkled brightly. It glittered like diamonds in the sunlight. Indeed, it glistened with all the colors of the rainbow.

The king was overjoyed. "What a magnificent gift!" he cried, jumping to his feet. "My dear man, how can I ever thank you?" He paused and thought for a moment. "I know!" he said at last. "I will give you a gift in return, one that is more precious, more valuable than anything in the entire world." And the king whispered instructions to his guard.

Soon the rich man, too, was asked to wait outside the door, and soon he, too, was handed a pouch to take home. He was so curious, so eager to see his gift, that he could hardly wait to leave the palace. Outside in the street he opened the pouch and reached in to pull out the most valuable gift that the king could find to give him.

That is when the rich man found himself holding his neighbor's rusty plate.

Egypt: Oral Tradition

THERE ONCE WAS A WITCH IN THE LAND OF LEMEN WHO LOVED TO PLAY AWFUL TRICKS IN THE MIDDLE OF THE NIGHT. SHE TURNED NIGHTINGALES INTO CROWS, WHICH AWAKENED EVERYONE WITH THEIR CAWING.

· THE WITCH BARUSHA ·

There once was a witch in the land of Yemen who loved to play awful tricks in the middle of the night. She turned nightingales into crows, and they awakened everyone with their cawing. She turned roosters into foxes, and they ate up all the chickens in the henhouses. And do you know what she loved to do most of all? She loved to turn newborn babies into puppies!

Well, one dark night, one of the women of the village was about to give birth, so the witch Barusha decided to slip in through the window of that woman's house. She tried to open the window very quietly, but it squeaked a bit.

The husband was pacing up and down, waiting for the baby's birth, and when he heard that little squeak, he rushed into the room just in time to see the witch climb inside. He knew at once who she was and why she was there, so he didn't ask any questions. He just grabbed the witch and was about to throw her into the fire, when all at once, before his eyes, the witch turned herself into a broom.

Now, there was a neighbor lady who had come to help with the new baby's birth. And when that neighbor heard all the racket, she ran to find out what was happening.

"Why are you going to throw that fine broom into the fire?" she cried.

"This is no broom," the husband answered. "It is the witch Barusha. I caught her climbing in through the window to turn my child into a puppy!"

"Are you sure you weren't dreaming?" asked the neighbor. "That looks like an ordinary broom to me. Let's go and ask your wife what we should do." So the two went to ask his wife.

"Burn it by all means!" she shouted. "Why should we take a chance?"

But when the witch Barusha, who was now a broom, heard this from the next room, she quickly turned herself into a pitcher and put a real broom in the place where she had been. When the man came back, he snatched up the broom and threw it into the fire. He watched until he saw that every last straw had been burned. Then he felt much better, certain that the witch was gone for good.

Just then he heard the first cries of his new baby, and he rushed into the bedroom to see his beautiful son and to kiss his wife. The man was very proud and happy, especially since he had kept the evil witch away from his child.

But by now the new mother was very thirsty. "Please, can you give me a cup of water?" she asked the neighbor lady. So the neighbor went into the other room and brought back the pitcher that was the witch Barusha. She poured a cup of water and gave it to the mother to drink. Then she and the man left the room so the mother and child could sleep.

Now, as soon as the woman closed her eyes, the witch Barusha changed herself from a pitcher into a black cat and crept toward the bed where the baby was sleeping at his mother's side. The cat crept closer, closer, closer, not making a sound—and just as it was about to pounce, the mother opened her eyes and started to scream. "Help! Help! Come quickly!" Her husband and the neighbor rushed into the room, just in time to see the cat only an arm's length from the newborn child.

The man grabbed the cat. It hissed and yowled and tried to scratch him, but the man refused to let go. He carried it to the fireplace and was about to throw it in when the cat began to speak. "Please, please," it begged, "let me go and I will give you a great reward. I swear I won't do you any harm."

Now, the man knew that a witch is bound to keep any promise she makes, so he said, "First return to your true shape." And all at once the witch Barusha was standing beside him, looking very frightened.

"You deserve to die in the fire," said the man, "but I will let you go if you vow never to harm a hair of any of my children. And that is not all. On the first birthday of every one of my children, I want you to leave a great gift in the hollow tree outside our house. If you do not, I will find you, no matter where you are, and cast you into the flames!"

When she heard these words, the witch Barusha shivered in fright and vowed to do exactly as the man had said. Then she climbed out the window and hurried away.

The man and his wife never saw the witch Barusha again, but on their son's first birthday, they found a bag of gold in the hollow tree outside their house. They used the money to rebuild their home, and soon it was the finest in the village. And they put bars on the windows so that no witches or other wicked creatures could climb inside.

In the years that followed, the man and his wife had twelve children, and each and every one received a bag of gold. Thus they became very rich, and the witch Barusha kept her promise and never harmed a hair of their heads. And they all lived happily ever after.

Yemen: Oral Tradition

SABBATH CLOTHES. SO TOO DID THE RAGS SHE WAS WEARING TURN INTO A MAGNIFICENT DRESS. THE BOYS LOOKED AT ONE ANOTHER IN AMAZEMENT, AND THAT IS WHEN THEY DISCOVERED THAT THEY TOO WERE DRESSED IN THE FINEST

M. IOFIN 1996

· THE SABBATH WALKING STICK ·

Long ago, in the faraway land of Turkey, three brothers lived together in a tiny house. The eldest was very strong and could leap all the way to the top of a tree. The second loved to eat and stuffed his pockets with every wild fruit and nut he found in the forest. The third was both clever and kind, sharing his food with anyone he met and caring for animals that were hurt.

Now, the brothers were orphans, so they had to take care of themselves. All week long they worked hard, collecting wood to sell in the village and doing their chores at home. They saved their pennies, and on the eve of the Sabbath, they bought bread and fish for a festive dinner.

One Friday, the brothers were gathering wood deep in the forest, when they suddenly remembered that it was almost time for the Sabbath, and they had not made any preparations. They started to hurry home, but before long realized they were lost—and the sun was about to set!

The boys ran this way and that, searching for the way home. They were terrified that they might have to spend the night in the forest, with wild beasts lurking about.

Then the brothers spotted a little cottage almost hidden by trees. They knocked at the door, and it was opened by an old woman dressed in rags. When they told her they were lost, she invited them in. "You are welcome to stay the night," she said, and her voice was kind.

The boys were very grateful to have found a place to stay, but still they looked sad. And when the old woman asked them why, they said it was because they missed celebrating the Sabbath. "Oh, I was about to do that myself," she said. "Won't you join me?" The boys said that yes, of course they would. But where, they wondered, were the Sabbath candles and the other preparations for the Sabbath meal?

Just then the old woman picked up her walking stick and waved it three times. A white linen cloth appeared out of the air and spread itself upon the table. And before their very eyes, two silver candlesticks appeared holding white candles, along with a *challah*, a silver cup, and a flask of wine. The rags she was wearing turned into a beautiful Sabbath dress. The boys looked at one another in amazement, and they discovered that they too were dressed in the finest Sabbath clothes.

The old woman lit the candles and said the Sabbath blessings. The boys watched in wonder as she waved the walking stick three more times, and all sorts of good things to eat appeared on the table: fish, chicken and rice, and sweet honey cakes for dessert.

So it was that the brothers spent a wonderful Sabbath in the old woman's cottage, listening to the tales she told and eating to their hearts' content. When the Sabbath was over, she waved the walking stick in the air, and all the things that had appeared vanished like smoke.

The old woman saw how amazed the boys were. "Would you like to have a magic walking stick of your own?" she asked.

"Oh, yes," they answered.

"Indeed, you may have mine," she said, "but only if you do as I ask." The boys quickly promised that they would.

"There is a stream not far from my hut," said the old woman, "and on the far side stands a large apple tree. Just bring me an apple from that tree and you shall have the magic stick." That seemed simple enough to the boys, but then the old woman added: "But it must be the right apple." Yet when the boys asked which one that might be, the old woman refused to say any more about it.

The next morning, the first brother strode across the stream and found the apple tree. Its branches were heavy with the most beautiful red apples he had ever seen. "Which is the right one?" he asked himself. "Probably the one that is hardest to get." So in one leap he jumped to the uppermost branch of the tree, and picked the apple right on top. Then he hurried back to the stream, where he noticed a lovely butterfly flapping its wings. "Give me the apple," it fluttered.

"An apple? What would you do with an apple?" asked the first brother.

He waved the butterfly away and crossed the stream. When he reached the old woman's house, he proudly handed her the apple.

"I'm sorry," she said. "This is not the right apple." She mumbled a magic spell and suddenly the first brother found himself back at home, frozen to one spot, unable to move.

Then the second brother set out, and after he crossed the stream and found the tree, he, too, asked himself, "Which is the right apple?" They all looked so good that he decided to pick as many as he could carry, and he stuffed his pockets until they were full. Now those apples were very fine, and he couldn't resist eating one after another, and by the time he reached the stream, there was only one left.

As he waded across, a butterfly flapped its wings and fluttered, "Give me your apple."

"Don't be silly," said the second brother. "I need it." Soon he was back at the old woman's house and he handed the last apple to her. But she refused to take it. "I'm sorry," she said. "This is not the right apple." Again she mumbled the magic spell, and the second brother found himself back at home, frozen to one spot, unable to move hand or foot—just like his elder brother.

It was time for the third brother to try his luck. He, too, crossed the stream and found the apple tree. "Which is the right one?" he asked himself. He finally chose a large red apple that had fallen from the tree, because he didn't want to pick one that was still growing.

When he returned to the stream, a butterfly flapped its wings and fluttered, "Give me your apple." The third brother thought the butterfly looked hungry and sad, so he said, "If you need the apple, take it." And he held out the apple for the butterfly.

All at once, to the boy's amazement, the butterfly vanished, and in its place stood the old woman. "That is the right apple," she said with a gleam in her eye, and held out the Sabbath walking stick. The third brother took the stick and thanked her with all his heart. Then the old woman pronounced another spell, and the third brother found himself standing in front of his own hut.

At that very moment his two brothers were released from the spell and ran out to greet him. They had learned their lesson and vowed never to be greedy again. So too did they all celebrate the old woman's gift, for they knew that the Sabbath walking stick was precious indeed.

From then on, the three brothers used the stick each week, bringing forth a fine Sabbath table filled with tasty food. They always invited others who were poor and hungry to share in their Sabbath meals, and they never forgot the old woman who had given them such a wonderful gift.

Turkey: Oral Tradition

"Amsha is so heavy," said the old woman, "that not even the earth can hold him up. If he doesn't wear his magic shoes, he sinks into the ground. Now, if you can take one of his shoes and hide it, then he will do anything you ask in order to get his shoe back."

· AMSHA THE GIANT ·

nce upon a time there was a poor woodcutter who had two children, and their names were Reuben and Rachel. They were so poor that they owned only the little hut in which they lived and the goat that gave them their milk and cheese.

Every day the woodcutter would go to the forest to cut wood, and every day Reuben and Rachel would lead the goat to a nearby field and tie its rope to a tree. And the children would play while the goat nibbled grass.

One day the goat was restless. She pulled her rope so hard that it broke, and she dashed off into the forest. The children ran after her as fast as they could, knowing that if they didn't catch the goat, they would have nothing to eat or drink. But the goat ran even faster, and soon the children were lost in the forest, with no goat in sight.

Rachel began to cry. "Don't worry," said Reuben, who wanted to comfort her, "we'll find our way back." He looked around for a familiar tree, or path, or bush—something that would show him how to get home. But all he could see was the dense forest. By now the sun was beginning to set, and it was getting dark. Soon the animals would begin to prowl about.

"Come, Rachel," he said, "we must find something to eat and a place to sleep." As he led her through the trees, they saw a bush filled with ripe berries! They circled the bush, picking and eating until their fingers were purple with berry juice. It was then that they discovered the entrance to a cave, hidden behind the bush. "Quick, Rachel," Reuben said. "Let's go in. It will be safe inside the cave when night falls."

Now, the cave was dark and cool and scary, but the children huddled together, and soon they fell asleep.

In the morning, when the children awoke, Rachel noticed a faint light at the far end of the cave. "Look, Reuben," she said, pointing it out, "maybe we can get out of the forest that way."

Now, it was very hard for Rachel and Reuben to make their way through that cave, for the ceiling was quite low, and they had to walk bent over, feeling for jagged rocks. Ever so slowly they moved along, and as they did, the light became brighter.

Finally they reached the end of the cave and stepped out into the open air. And what did they see? Great grassy fields stretched before them. They had left the forest behind, but here and there stood trees like nothing Reuben and Rachel had ever seen before. The trees were gigantic, and the berry bushes that grew beneath them held berries as big as oranges.

Reuben and Rachel walked all day, looking for someone to help them find their way home. And just before sunset, they saw an enormous house, built between two sandy hills.

"Who could live in a house that big?" Reuben gasped. At first he was afraid to knock on the huge door. But as it grew darker, Reuben decided that he must. So he gathered up his courage and knocked with his fist, for the knocker was far above his head.

The door opened, and towering above them was an enormous old woman. At first the children were frightened to see someone so big, but then they saw that her face was kind. As for the old woman, she was surprised to see two young children in that faraway place.

"How did you come here?" she asked, and the children told their tale.

"I'm sorry, but you can't stay here," she said. "My son, Amsha, is a giant and he's always hungry. If he sees you, he will gobble you up in a single bite!"

Rachel began to cry, "Let's run away, Reuben!" But Reuben turned to the old woman. "Please help us," he begged. "Isn't there some way we can be safe from the giant?"

"Well, there is one thing you can do, if you are brave," said the old woman. "You could hide under Amsha's bed, and when he is asleep, you could steal one of his shoes."

Now, you may wonder why stealing one of the giant's shoes would keep the children safe. The truth is that those shoes were magic shoes.

"Amsha is so heavy," said the old woman, "that not even the earth can hold him up. If he doesn't wear his magic shoes, he sinks into the ground. If you hide one of his shoes, then he will do anything you ask in order to get it back. And if you can make him promise to help you, you need not be afraid that he will break his promise, for if he does, the magic of his shoes will be lost forever."

Reuben and Rachel thanked the old woman for her advice and for the food she gave them. Then they hid beneath the giant's bed.

No sooner were they out of sight than they heard a thump so loud it sounded like thunder. It was the giant knocking at the door, and the old woman let him in. Peeking out from under the bed, the children saw that he was as tall as a mighty tree and towered far above his old mother.

"Mother, I smell human blood," he roared.

"Now, now," said his mother, "two children came to the door today, but I told them to run for their lives before you came home."

"Why did you do that?" shouted the giant. "Don't you know how hungry I am?"

"If you are so hungry, just sit down and eat your supper," said his mother. So Amsha forgot about the children and ate the huge meal his mother had prepared. After he had eaten his fill, he took off his shoes, lay down on his bed, and fell asleep.

As soon as the children heard the giant snoring, they crawled out from under the bed and dragged one of his shoes to the front door—but the handle was too high for them to reach.

Then they heard someone coming. What could they do? They jumped into the shoe and hid inside it. But it was only the old woman, who had come to help.

A moment later, the big door creaked open, and the old woman set the shoe out on the doorstep with the children still inside it.

"Good luck," she whispered as she closed the door.

"Thank you," they whispered back. Then they climbed out of the shoe and dragged it as far from the house as they could.

Reuben and Rachel spent hours covering the shoe with sand. For shovels, they used two giant spoons that the old woman had given them. Then they made a hole in the sand and climbed back inside the shoe. Oh, it made a warm house on that cold night!

Now, when Amsha the giant awoke the next morning, the first thing he did was to reach for his magic shoes. And when he found only one, he shouted, "Mother, where's my other shoe? What happened to my shoe?"

"I don't know," she answered. "Look for it yourself."

So the angry giant put on the one shoe and hopped about, looking first inside the house, then outside, near where the other shoe was hidden. But he didn't find a thing. Soon the exhausted giant cried, "Oh, I would give anything to have my shoe back!"

As soon as Reuben heard this, he crawled out of the sand-covered shoe and stood as tall as he could before the giant. "I know where your shoe can be found," he called up to Amsha, "but I won't tell you—unless you promise to help us get back home."

The giant was surprised to see the brave little boy standing there, but he was also tired of standing on one foot, so he quickly agreed. "I promise to help you get home, and I won't harm you."

Then Reuben called to his sister, "Rachel, come out. We must show the giant his shoe." They pointed to the mound of sand where it was hidden, and Amsha dug up his shoe, poured out the sand and put it on.

After that, the giant felt so much better that he shared his breakfast with the children and filled their pockets with jewels from his giant trunk. Then he picked them up, put them on his shoulder, and set out for their home.

Now, the fastest way home was through the cave. But Amsha could never fit inside it, so he had to take a different way, which was many miles longer. But the distance passed quickly because each of the giant's steps was three miles long.

When the children's father felt the earth shake, he came running to see what had happened, and there on the shoulder of a giant he saw his Reuben and Rachel, smiling as they rode along.

The giant set the children down, and their father ran to them and hugged and kissed them. Then they all thanked Amsha many times. As for the giant, he left with a smile on his face, for he had grown to like the children very much. Besides, this was his first good deed, and he rather liked the feeling of it.

So it was that Reuben and Rachel and their father were reunited. And they were never poor again, for the jewels that the giant had given the children were enough to buy a thousand goats.

Iraq: Oral Tradition

THE KING HAS TWO HORNS! "Two Horns! THE KING HAS TWO HORNS!" AND THE SONG WAS PICKED UP BY THE WIND, AND WAS CARRIED OVER THE MOUNTAINS, AND BEFORE LONG IT WAS HEARD BY THE PEOPLE OF THE CITY; AND THEY BEGAN TO WHISPER AMONG THEMSELVES,

· THE KING'S SECRET ·

Long ago, in the land of Morocco, there lived a king who had a terrible problem: growing out of each side of his head was a huge horn. The king was so ashamed. He was afraid that if people knew about those horns, they would laugh at him, and he would lose their respect.

So for many years the king didn't cut his hair. He let it grow and grow and grow until it looked like a forest. But finally the king could bear it no longer, so he called for a barber to cut his hair.

This the barber did, but no sooner did he finish his job than the king had him locked up in prison. For that way the barber could not tell anyone the king's secret. And the next time the king needed to have his hair cut, he called upon another barber. And that barber, too, was sent to prison.

Things went on this way for a number of years, until at last there was only one barber left in the land, a Jewish barber, who had not yet cut the king's hair. The king thought, "If I imprison this barber, who will be left to cut my hair?"

So he called for the barber to appear before him. "You shall be my own royal barber," he said, "and I shall give you great rewards and make you a member of my court—if you promise to keep my secret. But if you tell my secret to anyone, anyone at all, I shall lock you in prison and throw away the key!"

"Oh, your majesty, I give you my word," said the barber. "I'll never tell your secret to anyone. But what is the secret?"

"I would rather not speak about it," said the king. "When you cut my hair, you will know."

So the barber began to cut the king's hair. And when he did, he saw the horns, one on each side of the king's head. He silently gasped, "Two horns!

Two horns! The king has two horns!" But, of course, he said nothing.

Every month the barber went back to the king's private chambers, and every month he cut the king's hair. And every time he did so, he looked at those horns and thought to himself, "Two horns! Two horns! The king has two horns!" But naturally he said nothing.

Yet, as month after month went by, it became harder and harder for the barber to keep the secret. One day he was sitting at the dinner table when he started to say, "Two horns! Two horns! The k . . ." Fortunately, he caught himself in time.

Then one night, while he was asleep, he began to snore, "Two horns! Two horns! The k . . ." Luckily, he woke up in time.

Then one morning, as he was singing in his bathtub, he began to sing, "Two horns! Two horns! The k . . ." He just managed to stop himself in time.

Now the barber began to worry. He could no longer keep the secret to himself. But if the secret should get out. . . . He shuddered to think of what would happen to him. What could the poor barber do?

Then one day, while he was cutting the king's hair, the barber hummed a tune to himself, a melody his mother had sung to him when he was a boy. It was about how the Jews who lived in the Holy Land would confide their secrets to the Wailing Wall in Jerusalem, where only God could hear them. That was it! In a flash the barber knew that he had found the solution: he would tell his secret to a wall.

So the barber left the palace and ran through the city. He ran far away, way out into the country. He passed through forests and villages, crossed mountains and valleys, swam rivers and streams. At last he found a huge cave with reeds growing at its entrance. He ran to the very end of the cave, and stood facing the back wall. Surely there, so far away from the city, no one could hear him. And the barber shouted as loudly as he could, "Two horns! Two horns! The king has two horns!"

"Two horns. Two horns." The words echoed throughout the cave.

"Ah," sighed the barber with relief. He felt much better. Yes, he had gotten rid of the secret at last.

As he left the cave, the barber noticed two apple trees growing in the field outside, one tree with green apples and one tree with red ones. The apples looked so fine that he filled his pouch with some of each kind and took them with him. Then he went back, through the rivers and streams, past the mountains and valleys, past the forests and villages, right through the streets of the city until he returned to the palace. He was very happy! And in the months that followed, he continued to cut the king's hair.

Time passed. But one day a shepherd boy wandered by that cave and saw some beautiful reeds growing there. "Oh, these reeds will make a fine flute for me to play while I watch my sheep," he thought. So he plucked one of the reeds, cut it in half, and made a flute. But the moment the shepherd boy played it for the first time, the flute began to sing, "Two horns! Two horns! The king has two horns!" And every time the shepherd boy played the flute thereafter, he heard the same words, for that was the only song the flute could play.

Before long all the trees in the forest heard that song, and they too sang, "Two horns! Two horns! The king has two horns!" And the birds of the forest began to chirp, "Two horns! Two horns! The king has two horns!" And the song was picked up by the wind, and was carried over the mountains, and before long it was heard by the people of the city. And they began to whisper among themselves, "Two horns! Two horns! The king has two horns!"

Soon the king heard what the people were saying, and he was horrified. He was certain that the barber must have revealed the secret, for everyone else who knew about it was locked away in prison. The furious king shouted, "Guards, go to the home of the barber to arrest him!"

Now, the barber had also heard the whisperings of the people, but he could not understand how the secret had gotten out. And so when he saw the guards arriving at his door, the barber was terrified, for he knew that prison awaited him. With no time to make any preparations, he grabbed his pouch—just before the guards broke down his door and dragged him off to prison.

The king was so angry that he ordered the guards not to feed the barber for a month. And in his lonely cell, the barber was afraid he would starve to death. Then he remembered the apples he had thrown into his pouch, the ones from the trees outside the cave. He opened the pouch and, much to his delight, saw that the apples seemed as fresh and crisp as ever. He took a bite out of one of the green ones, but then, to his horror, he felt something growing out of his head. Feeling with his hands, he discovered that he too now had two horns! Horns as big as those of the king!

Nothing that had ever happened to the barber—not even being thrown into the dungeon without food—was as terrible as those horns. He threw the rest of the apple away, even though he was still hungry, and he wept.

But the next day he was still very hungry, and this time he took a bite out of one of the red apples—he certainly was not going to eat the green ones anymore! But no sooner did he bite into the red apple than he felt a strange sensation on his head, and when he reached up, he was amazed to discover that the horns were gone! He felt his head again and again—it was true, the horns were gone!

At that moment the barber knew what he had to do. He grabbed the pouch with the apples and ran to the door, calling, "Guard, guard, take me to the king at once. I know how to get rid of his horns."

The king reluctantly agreed to see him. "If this is a trick, my dear barber, know that your head will not remain on your shoulders much longer, for you have made me the laughingstock of the land."

The barber knew it would be useless to explain, so he simply took one of the red apples out of his pouch and handed it to the king. "Take a bite of this apple, your Majesty," the barber said. And as soon as the king bit into the apple, his horns disappeared. The king felt his head with his hands. Then he ran to the mirror and studied his head from every angle. The horns were gone! Weeping with joy, the king hugged the barber and thanked him again and again and assured him that he would always be a wealthy man.

Then the king had the barber cut his hair very short, and he ordered a grand procession to pass before all the citizens of the city. And the king led the procession himself, so everyone could see that he did not have horns.

When the king returned to the palace, he kept his word and rewarded the barber with seven bags of gold. Then he released every other barber from prison and sent them all happily back to their homes.

In the years that followed, the king ruled his land with wisdom and mercy, and never again was anyone in the kingdom ever heard saying, "Two horns! Two horns! The king has two horns!"

Morocco: Oral Tradition

· THE FISHERMAN AND THE SILVER FISH ·

Once upon a time, there was a poor Jewish fisherman who had been fishing all day without any luck. He was just about to go home empty-handed when, all of a sudden, he caught a very large fish. It was the largest and most beautiful fish he had ever seen, with silver scales that shone in the sun and eyes that looked ancient and wise. The fisherman was imagining how much money such a fish would bring him when, to his astonishment, the fish began to speak: "Please, kind sir, set me free, and I will see to it that you are richly rewarded."

The fisherman could hardly believe his ears. How could a fish speak? He wasn't about to let such a fine catch go. "How is it possible that you can speak?" he asked. "And what kind of reward do you mean? I could sell you to the king for two gold pieces."

"The reward I offer you could be worth much more than that," replied the fish. "And it was Moses who gave me the ability to speak."

Now the fisherman was even more amazed. "Are you that old?" he asked.

"Yes," said the fish, "I was present at the crossing of the Red Sea. When the waters parted and the people began to cross, there was a crippled boy who could not cross on his own. His mother and father could not help him because they had their hands full, carrying younger children. So Moses called upon me to carry the boy across the sea on my back. I did as Moses asked, and as a reward, Moses asked God to give me the great blessings of long life and speech. And that is why I have lived for so long and how I am able to speak to you."

Now, when the poor fisherman heard this story, he realized that it must be true, for he himself heard the great fish speak. Still, he was reluctant to let it go. "I believe you," he said, "but I am a poor man, and my wife will never forgive me if I release you and receive nothing in return. What is it that you have to offer me?"

"Make a wish," the fish said, "and I will call upon Moses to call upon God for you, and surely God will grant your wish."

The fisherman thought for a while. Then he said, "I am tired of being a poor fisherman who can barely support his family. I would like to have a job in the king's palace."

The fish answered, "Set me free, and I will do everything in my power to see that your wish comes true. And if you ever need me again, just come back to this same place and call for me, and I will come to you."

So the fisherman set the silver fish free, and it swam away into the depths of the ocean. And all the way home the fisherman wondered if he had done the right thing by letting the fish go.

Meanwhile, the fish called upon Moses: "Moses, remember how I helped at the crossing of the Red Sea? Now I seek a favor of you. I ask you to ask God to grant the wish of a poor fisherman."

And so Moses called upon God to help the fisherman, but the Lord replied, "Moses, my son, do not interfere with things that don't concern you. Leave this poor man alone—let him live as he was." But Moses reminded God of how the silver fish had helped him, and he begged God to answer his request. At last God agreed to help the poor fisherman.

Early the next morning, before the fisherman had gone down to the shore to fish, there was a knock at his door. When the fisherman opened it, he saw one of the king's guards standing there, and he was frightened. The guard said, "Last night the king dreamed that he who lived in this cottage, next to the sea, was a very wise man indeed. And so the king is calling upon you to come to the palace and serve as his vizier. Of course, you should bring your family with you."

When the poor fisherman heard this wonderful news, he could hardly believe his luck, and his wife and children jumped up and down with joy. The guard brought them back to the palace, where they were given fine clothes and a house of their own, and then the fisherman appeared before the king. When the king saw him, he stepped off his throne and said: "Yes, that is the very man I saw in my dream. Surely you are the wisest man in all this land, and I intend to make you my vizier."

The fisherman bowed low before the king, and promised that he would always do his best to serve him well. He understood that the silver fish had fulfilled his promise and that this great blessing had come to him because he had set the fish free.

Now, the very next day the king came to the fisherman and asked him a very difficult question: "Tell me, my wise vizier, should I go to war with the neighboring kingdom or should I not?" The fisherman asked for one day's time to think over this question, and then he hurried to the place on the shore where he had caught the silver fish. He called for the fish:

Silver fish, silver fish,
Silver fish in the sea.
Silver fish, silver fish,
Please come to me.

All at once the fish appeared. "Why have you called upon me?" asked the fish. "Did you not receive the reward that you asked for?"

"Yes, yes, I have been rewarded. The king has made me his vizier. But now he has asked me to give him my advice, and I do not know how to answer him." He told the fish about the king's problem.

"Tell the king to send ten precious gifts to his enemy, and to offer his hand in friendship," the fish replied, "for peace is always better than war."

The fisherman who was now the king's vizier thanked the fish for this advice and hurried back to the palace. The next morning he repeated what the fish had told him. The king replied, "That is very wise advice, indeed. Let us try it and see what happens."

So the king sent ten precious gifts to his enemy. Not long afterward, his couriers returned—bearing even more gifts than they had delivered! The king's enemy was now his friend, and the peace between them would last for a long, long time.

When the king saw this, he realized how wise he had been to seek out the fisherman to be his vizier. From then on, the king sought his advice on every important matter. As for the fisherman, he, of course, always turned to the silver fish for advice, and the fish never let him down. In this way several years passed, and the vizier was well-respected, and his family had everything they desired.

One day the fisherman's wife said to him, "You know, the king turns to you for his every decision. He would be lost without you. The truth is that you are already king in everything but name. Why don't you go back to that talking fish and ask to be made king? Then I would be the queen, and your children would be the prince and princess."

The fisherman was really quite happy with his lot, but his wife nagged at him every day, and before long he began to think that she might be right. After all, he was already doing the work of the king, so why shouldn't he serve as king himself? At last he went back to the shore, and once again he called the fish:

> Silver fish, silver fish,
> Silver fish in the sea.
> Silver fish, silver fish,
> Please come to me.

The fish appeared, as before. "What has the king asked of you now?" he asked.

"That is not why I have called you," said the fisherman. "Ever since I became the vizier, the king has let me make his every decision. All the advice you have given me has turned out well. But my wife thinks that since I already do the work of the king, I should be the king myself. So I have come to ask you to ask Moses for help in making me king."

"Are you sure that is what you want?" asked the fish.

"Yes," said the fisherman, "that is what I want—to be king."

And the fish replied, "I will call upon Moses to see what the Holy One can do for you."

Then the fish swam off into the sea and was gone.

Now it happened that on that very night the king died in his sleep, and when the people learned this, they shed tears of grief—for the king had no son to take his place. Then the king's advisors turned to the fisherman and said: "The king trusted your wisdom more than that of anyone else. We too have grown to trust you, and we would like you to be our king." The fisherman agreed to their request, and soon a coronation was held, and he was crowned in the presence of all the people.

Now the fisherman had all the wealth and power he could ever wish for, and he still had the fish to guide him. With its good advice, all his decisions were wise ones, and the people of that kingdom enjoyed great peace and abundance. Everyone was happy—everyone, that is, except the fisherman's wife. True, she was the queen now, and her son and daughter were the prince and princess, but she wanted more.

She complained to her husband, and he said, "Is it not enough that I am the king and you are the queen? What more do you want?"

"We are the king and queen of this kingdom, but there is still the rest of the world," she answered.

The fisherman said, "Only God is the ruler of the world."

"That is true," said his wife, "but don't you want to know what it's like to be God?"

Even though it seemed like an impossible request, the fisherman thought, "My wife is right. I am a wise king and I make important decisions every day. But God makes even more decisions and rules over a greater kingdom. I wonder what it would be like to be God."

So he went back to the shore and called upon the silver fish:

Silver fish, silver fish,
Silver fish in the sea.
Silver fish, silver fish,
Please come to me.

And when the fish arrived, it asked, "What is it that you would like to know?"

The fisherman replied, "I don't need advice today, but I do have one last request."

"Don't you already rule the kingdom?" asked the fish. "What more could you possibly want?"

And the fisherman said: "I want to know what it is like to rule the world."

"Only God can rule the world," said the ancient fish.

"But I want to know what it is like to be such a great ruler. I want to know what God does all day."

"Are you sure?" asked the silver fish. And when the fisherman who was now the king insisted that he was, the fish said, "I will call upon Moses to see what can be done for you. Come back tomorrow and I will tell you whether God has decided to honor your request."

The silver fish swam away and was gone. Soon after, it called upon Moses and told him what the fisherman wanted, and Moses, in turn, told God.

God replied, "Moses, Moses, I did what you asked. I answered all the man's requests. I made him the king's vizier, and then I made him king. But I told you from the first that you should not interfere in such matters. I created my people, and I decree who will be wealthy and who will be poor. But I want you to see how this request turns out. Therefore, go back and tell this man that tomorrow morning he will see with his own eyes what I do all day."

So Moses related God's words to the ancient fish, and the fish told the fisherman, "Very well, tomorrow you will see with your own eyes what the Creator of the world does all day." And when the fisherman heard these words, his joy was without measure.

That night the king slept soundly. But in the morning when he opened his eyes, he found, to his dismay, that he was dressed in the clothes of a poor man and was lying on a mattress of straw. In the corner were his wife and children, also wearing rags.

"What happened to me?" cried the poor man. "Is this a dream? Only yesterday I was the king, living in the palace."

He ran outside, straight to the shore, and called upon the silver fish. And when the fish appeared, the man fell upon his knees and cried, "What did God do to me? Why did this happen? Make everything as it was yesterday."

"I'm sorry," said the fish. "God did not do this to you. You yourself asked to know what the Creator does all day, and God answered your request. Every day God raises some people to riches, while others have their station in life lowered. That is God's work. That is what God does all day."

And with these words, the fish swam away, never to be seen again.

Morocco: Oral Tradition

"MY SON," THE KING WOULD OFTEN SAY, "YOU MUST BE ABLE TO EARN A LIVING IN A TIME OF NEED OR DANGER. MONEY MAY COME AND MONEY MAY GO, BUT A PROFESSION LASTS A LIFETIME."

· The Weaving that Saved the Prince ·

There once was a prince who loved to play games with his friends and dream of the day when he would rule the kingdom. But his father, the king, insisted that the boy learn a trade as well. "My son," he would often say, "you must be able to earn a living in times of need or danger. Money may come and money may go, but a profession lasts a lifetime."

Now, the boy did not fully understand the meaning of his father's words, but he obeyed his wishes and began to study a trade. And what trade did the prince choose? He chose to be a weaver of carpets.

The boy was very clever, so he quickly learned how to weave carpets of varied colors, decorated with letters and intricate patterns. After the prince had become a master weaver, his father, the king, rewarded him with a precious gift—a noble horse. The prince rejoiced greatly over this gift, and he began to practice riding, until he became a rider whose ability was without equal.

One day, as the prince galloped on his horse into the desert surrounding the kingdom, he stumbled upon a region where thieves lived, hidden in caves. Now, when the thieves saw the young man approaching, they decided to steal his horse. But after they had captured the horse, the thieves were afraid that the young man might give away the location of their caves, so they decided they would have to kill him.

The prince recognized from the first that he was in danger, and he knew that he had to keep his true identity a secret. It was then that he recalled the craft he had learned.

"Surely you can use more money," he told the thieves. "I am a skilled weaver, so I should be worth more to you alive than dead. For as long as you let me live, I will continue to weave beautiful carpets for you—beautiful carpets worthy of a king."

The thieves held a discussion among themselves. "If his carpets are really beautiful and fetch a good price," they whispered, "we will keep this boy here as our slave." Out loud they declared, "Very well, we will let you weave one carpet, and we will see if what you say is true."

Meanwhile, the king and queen began to worry about their missing son. When a day had passed with no word from him, they knew that the boy must be in danger. The king immediately sent a hundred of his troops to search for the prince, but all their efforts were in vain, for they knew nothing about the caves. Then the king proclaimed that a great reward would be given to whoever discovered what had happened to the prince. But days and weeks passed, and still there was no clue to his fate.

In the meantime, the prince told his captors to bring him a loom and silk threads of many colors, and he promised that within a month he would finish weaving a splendid carpet—worthy of the palace of the king. Thus the threads were brought to him, and the prince set to work. Hour after hour, day after day, the boy sat at the loom, weaving from dawn to dusk, with only pita and water to sustain him.

It was a very elaborate carpet that he wove, filled with flowers and letters and patterns of all kinds. The clever prince also wove a crown among its many decorations—just like the one his father wore—and a hidden map, showing the location of the thieves' hideout.

The prince plied his craft with great speed, and when the carpet was completed, it astounded the thieves who beheld it. Never had they seen anything so magnificent. They knew it would bring them a fortune. At first they planned to sell it in the marketplace, but the prince said, "Why not take it to the king's palace, for there you will surely receive the largest sum of money."

So two of the thieves hurried off to the king's palace. There the wondrous carpet was unrolled for the gatekeeper, who was dazzled by its beauty. Quickly he summoned the king's minister, who took the carpet straight to the king himself. The king, equally dazzled by the carpet's beauty, looked at it closely. As he did so, the crown, so like his own, caught his eye, and he knew that the carpet could have been woven only by the prince himself. Looking even more closely, he discovered the hidden map and realized what he had to do.

The thieves were delighted, of course, when the king's minister returned to the gate and handed them a bag of gold. They thanked him and took their leave. But as soon as they were gone, the king ordered his guards to set out to rescue the prince, using the map as their guide. As for the thieves, they were not expecting an attack, and thus they were quickly captured, and the prince was set free.

When he returned to the palace, the prince said to his father, "If not for your wisdom, Father, I would never have lived to see this day, for it was the trade you encouraged me to learn that saved me from a bitter fate."

Iraq: Oral Tradition

IT HAPPENED THAT ONE DAY AN OLD RABBI, ON HIS WAY HOME FROM SYNAGOGUE, SAT DOWN ON THE STEPS OF THAT HOUSE TO REST. HE WAS CARRYING HIS PRAYERBOOK AND BEGAN TO READ ONE OF THE PSALMS OUT LOUD. OF COURSE HE READ THE NAME OF GOD.

· A Family of Demons ·

There once was a father demon, a mother demon, and a little girl demon.

What did the demons look like? The father demon had the face of a monkey with one eye closed. One of his ears was very long, and the other was very short. The mother demon had the face of a goat, and, like a goat, she had a little beard. The little girl demon had the face of a duck, but her feet were like those of a cat.

Now, these demons weren't really evil. They just went up and down the streets of town having fun. One day they came to a large house where a little girl lived with her parents.

"Let's go into that house," said the father demon, "and live there for a while." So they did.

Inside the house, the father demon hid inside a bottle of wine. And when the cork was lifted, he jumped out, making a terrible noise and filling the room with smoke and lightning and thunder. The family shrieked and screamed, and afterward they found a pile of ashes on the floor. And even though they opened every window, the terrible smell lasted for days.

As for the mother demon, she loved to sneak around after dark, making strange noises outside windows. The children who heard these sounds hid under the covers all night and were afraid to fall asleep.

And what did the little girl demon do? She liked to hide inside mirrors. One day she entered the mirror of the little girl, who was just the same height as she was. So when the girl stood in front of the mirror, she saw the girl demon instead of herself.

The girl demon copied everything the girl did. When the girl shook her head, the girl demon shook her duck head. When the girl lifted her foot, the girl demon lifted her cat foot.

"Oh, no!" cried the girl, "I've turned into a strange creature!" She ran screaming to her mother and father, but they showed her in their own mirror that she was just the same as ever.

Now, the demon family was afraid of only one thing, and that was the Name of God. When people said their prayers or read the Bible, the demons shook with fear, for they knew that whenever anyone said God's Name, that Name had the power to make the demons disappear.

And so it happened that one day an old rabbi, on his way home from synagogue, sat down on the steps of that house to rest. He was carrying his prayer book and began to read one of the Psalms out loud. Of course he read the Name of God.

All at once the posts of the house began to tremble, and then the whole house began to shake. There was a great noise as if there were a storm inside. Just then the front door flew open, and the father demon, the mother demon, and the little girl demon rushed out as fast as they could. They didn't stop running until they had gone far, far away. And no one in that town ever heard of them again.

Eastern Europe: Nineteenth Century

THE KING DECLARED: "EACH OF YOU SHALL GET THE PAYMENT YOU DESERVE. NOW COME FORWARD AND EACH OF YOU MAY TAKE THE REWARD YOU FIND BESIDE YOUR PAINTING." AND THEY DID!

· THE ROYAL ARTISTS
AND THE CLEVER KING ·

nce a very rich king ordered his subjects to build a new palace. And when the palace was finished, he wanted the finest artist in all the land to paint beautiful pictures on its walls. But the king did not know which artist was the best.

What did he do? He called forth two of the most famous artists in all the land, and he bade each artist to paint one wall of a room in the palace. Between the artists he hung a dark curtain, so that neither one could see what the other was doing.

To each of the artists he said, "You have three months in which to paint a beautiful picture on the wall. At the end of that time I will choose the best picture, and the artist who painted that picture will be given the honor of decorating the other walls of my royal home—and he will receive a large bag of gold and jewels as well."

Now, one of the artists was talented and hard-working, and he set to work at once. Out came his brushes, his paints, and his palette, and soon he was humming as he worked. This artist hardly slept. He ate little, and did not drink the wine that the king sent him. He had no thoughts of the reward. Instead he thought only of his painting and of how to please the king.

But the other artist was lazy. Each day he remained in bed until noon. Then he ordered a pitcher of wine and a large meal, and as he ate and drank, he laughed out loud, "Ha! There is nothing better than the king's wine. That other artist is foolish! See how hard he works!" And not once did he paint a stroke upon the wall.

In this manner three months passed. The hard-working artist painted all day and all night. The lazy one did nothing.

But three days before the king was to look at their work, the lazy artist awoke and trembled. "I have done no work. I will be punished," he stammered. "What should I do?" And from that moment on he could neither eat nor drink nor sleep. One day passed, two, three—and he could not think of a plan.

Then, on the night before the arrival of the king, he got an idea. What did he do? The lazy artist brought a large bucket of black shiny oil, and brushed it on every part of the wall until it was as shiny as a mirror. Then he went to bed.

The next morning the king came to inspect the work of the two men. First he saw the painting of the hard-working artist. How magnificent it was! The birds looked so real that you could hear them chirping. The fruits looked so ripe that you wanted to reach out your hand to pluck them. The flowers looked so delicate that you could almost smell their fragrance.

The king was very pleased. He called upon the other members of his court, and they too gasped in delight, "We have never seen anything so wonderful!"

Then the king pulled the curtain and looked at the work of the lazy artist. It was exactly the same as the other, line for line, stroke for stroke. Yes, there were the same chirping birds, the same ripe fruit, the same fragrant flowers! The members of the court were even more astonished than before. "How can this be?" they gasped.

But the king, who was not so easily fooled, saw at once the difference between the work of the hard-working artist and that of the lazy one. And what did he do?

He took out just one large sack filled with gold and precious jewels. This he placed near the painting of the hard-working artist. At once all of those present saw the same bag of gold appear by the other wall, beside the lazy man's painting, and they realized it was only a reflection.

The king declared: "Each of you shall get the payment you deserve. Now, come forward and each of you take the reward you find beside your painting." And they did!

Eastern Europe: Nineteenth Century
A Tale of Rabbi Nachman of Bratzlav

THE TAILORS SAT DOWN TOGETHER TO TALK ABOUT MAKING THE COAT, BUT NO MATTER HOW HARD THEY TRIED, THEY COULDN'T FIGURE OUT HOW TO DO IT. THE PROBLEM WAS THAT THE MOON WAS SOMETIMES LITTLE AND SOMETIMES BIG.

· A Coat for the Moon ·

Once upon a time the moon came to the sun and said, "It isn't fair that you get to shine during the day when it's warm, while I have to shine at night when it's cold, especially in winter." The sun saw that the moon was unhappy, so he promised her, "I'll have a coat made to keep you warm."

So the sun called together all the big tailors of the city, who were rich, and asked them to make a coat for the moon—one that would keep her warm even on the coldest nights. The tailors sat down together to talk about making the coat, but no matter how hard they tried, they couldn't figure out how to do it. The problem was that the moon was sometimes little and sometimes big. And a coat that would fit when the moon was little would be too small when the moon was big. And a coat that would fit when the moon was big would be too big when the moon was little.

After a while the big tailors just gave up. They didn't know how to make a coat for the moon.

"Let us try!" begged the little tailors, who were poor. But when the big tailors heard this, they laughed out loud and said, "If we can't make a coat for the moon, how can you?"

But the little tailors were not about to give up. They talked and talked all night long. They too had many ideas, but no one could solve the problem of making a coat to fit the changing sizes of the moon.

And so they sat silently for a long time. At last one little tailor, whose name was Yankel, stood up. "What we need is a material that's very light, so that it can stretch. I have been thinking that the clouds in the sky would make a perfect coat for the moon."

Now the little tailors listened carefully, and they agreed that the clouds would be a good material, one that could stretch enough to be a coat for the moon. But then another tailor, whose name was Yosef, stood up looking puzzled. "But the clouds are high up in the sky. We'll never be able to climb high enough to reach them."

And all the little tailors nodded when they heard this, except Yankel. He stood up and cried, "I know how!"

"How?" they asked, all at the same time.

"Oh, it's not as hard as you think," Yankel explained. "Have you forgotten that sometimes clouds come down to earth? And when they do, they are called fog. Let's wait until a cloud comes down one day. When it does, we will be ready to cut and sew a coat for the moon. And then when the fog lifts and the cloud rises, it will surround the moon and keep her warm."

Now all the tailors stood up and clapped their hands. Yes, Yankel had shown them how to make a coat for the moon! And just think of what the big tailors would say when they learned that! So the little tailors rejoiced until one of them, who had a sour face, said, "Yes? And how can something as thin and light as a cloud keep the moon warm?" And when he said this, a hush fell upon the little tailors. The tailor with the sour face was right. The cloud wasn't heavy enough to be a coat for the moon!

So again the tailors sat down, their hands on their chins, thinking about how to solve the problem. Suddenly Yankel leaped to his feet, calling out, "I know how!"

"How?" they asked, all at the same time.

"We'll sew some stars into the cloud," he explained, "and those stars will keep the moon warm with their wonderful light."

The little tailors began to cheer when they heard these words, for Yankel had solved the problem once again. All the tailors thought so, except for the one with the sour face. He hushed everyone and said, in his sour voice, "Yes? And how are we going to get stars to sew into the cloud?" And when he said this, the smiles of the tailors turned to frowns, for they hadn't considered this problem.

Again there was a long silence. But Yankel was full of ideas that day, and at last he leaped up and cried, "I know how!"

"How?" they asked, all at the same time.

"Stars aren't to be found only in the sky," explained Yankel. "We all know that there are also stars floating in the river. Let's catch those stars and sew them into the fog!"

"Yes, yes, Yankel is a genius!" all the tailors shouted at the same time—all except, of course, the one with the sour face. He looked more sour than ever. "Yes?" he asked. "And how are you going to get the stars out of the river in order to sew them into the fog?"

The situation looked hopeless again. The little tailors were all worn out. Suddenly Yankel shouted "I know how!"

"How?" they asked, all at the same time.

"We'll all go together on a night when the fog rests near the shore of the river," Yankel answered, "and from our friends, the blacksmiths, we'll borrow bellows—those big pumps they use to make the fire blow higher. And we'll blow the fog into the river, where it will pick up the stars on its own. When the fog floats back up into the sky and becomes a cloud again, it will take the stars with it. And that way the moon will have a coat to keep her warm, even on the coldest nights!"

The little tailors jumped with joy, and not even the sour-faced tailor had anything to say. They all did just as Yankel said and waited for a night when a big cloud came down to earth as fog, and settled on the shore of the river.

That night, all the little tailors came together, carrying in their hands the bellows they had borrowed from their friends the blacksmiths. With the bellows they blew and blew and blew until they blew the fog over the river. And when it floated on the water, stars stuck to it on every side.

When the fog finally lifted and became a cloud again, the little tailors saw that it surrounded the moon on every side and that a cluster of stars could be seen surrounding her as well. It seemed to them that the moon was smiling that night. And why? At last she had a coat that could grow as big and small as she did—one that could keep her warm, even on the coldest nights.

Anyone who looks up into the sky will see it, for the moon wears that special coat to this very day!

Eastern Europe: Nineteenth Century
A Tale of Rabbi Nachman of Bratzlav

The Queen of the Sea (Egypt)

This story was previously unpublished. (IFA 8831, collected by Ronit Bronstein from Moni Tivoni.)

This is one of many stories that emphasize the importance of vows, which in the Jewish view are sacred and must be fulfilled. The Queen of the Sea sees to it that Daniel is saved and wishes for him to remain with her. But she lets him leave as long as he promises not to tell anyone where he has been. When he breaks that promise, his life in brought into danger. From this he learns the importance of remaining true to a vow.

The Enchanted Spring (France)

This is a story from the Jerusalem Talmud, Shabbat 6:8. This version is based on Mss Oxford Bodliani Or 135 (Hebrew). It is also found in *Hiddur ha-Ma'asiyot ve-Midrashot ve ha-Aggadot* (Hebrew) (Venice: 1551). The story is an early example of the nursery tale, "The Wolf and the Kids," in which a wolf pretends to be the father or mother of the kids in order to gain entry into their house.

This story demonstrates the compelling importance of giving charity, as well as the efforts that must be made to save someone who is in serious danger. Both of these are primary Jewish principles, found in the Bible, Talmud, and Midrash. In this case, the act of giving allows the rich man to save his own life, fulfilling the proverb that "Charity saves from death."

The Lamp on the Mountain (Turkey)

This story comes from *Hodesh Hodesh ve-Sippuro* 1976–1977, edited by Dov Noy (Jerusalem: Israel Folktale Archives, 1979). (IFA 11093, collected by Rachel Seri from Dina Elazar. AT 1262*A and AT 920*E.) There are several dozen variants of this tale collected by the Israel Folktale Archives (IFA) in Haifa.

This is a story about justice. It echoes the famous biblical story of how King Solomon determined the true mother of a child claimed by two women. Here the young Solomon realizes that the poor man has been cheated, and finds a clever way to prove his point. Justice, of course, is an essential Jewish principle, as demonstrated in the passage from Deuteronomy: "Justice, justice shall you pursue" (Deut. 16:20).

The Underground World (Palestine)

This story comes from Seder Rabbah Bereshit 31, edited by Solomon A. Wertheimer in *Battei Midrashot I*, pages 1–31, published in 1893. The underground world of Tevel is described in the Midrash.

This story about King Solomon and the man from Tevel, in which each of the two heads tries to set out in a different direction, serves as an allegory about people's inability to agree with each other. It teaches that we must cooperate with each other in order to achieve our goals. This is very much a Jewish ideal. Solomon teaches the two-headed son of the man from Tevel that he cannot cut himself off from his other head any more than we can cut ourselves off from other human beings.

The story also illustrates how some people want more than their share of wealth.

The Demon in the Wine Cellar (Yemen)

This story is from *Sippure Baale-hayim Yisrael* (Hebrew), edited by Dov Noy (Haifa: Israel Folktale Archives, 1978). (IFA 107, collected by Heda Jason from Yeffet Shvili.)

This story, too, demonstrates the importance of justice in Jewish life, where even the demon in the bottle agrees to have his case brought before a judge. In the Jewish view, when two parties cannot find a way to agree on an important matter, they seek the decision of a judge, usually a rabbi or a rabbinical court.

The Rusty Plate (Egypt)

This is a story from the Israel Folktale Archives. (IFA 2871, collected by Ilana Zohar from her mother, Flora Cohen.)

This story emphasizes the Jewish idea that what matters most to God is what is in a person's heart. This is closely connected to the concept of *kavvanah* in prayer, in which a person's spiritual intention—not the outward appearance—is what really matters. Here the rusty plate proves to be an acceptable gift because of the assistance of Elijah, who, as God's messenger, comes to the poor man's assistance because the man's intentions are good.

The Witch Barusha (Yemen)

This story comes from *Hadre Teman* (Hebrew), edited by Nissim Binyamin Gamlieli (Tel Aviv: Afikim, 1978). (IFA 11525, collected by Nissim Binyamin Gamlieli from Yeshuah ben Yosef David. AT 313H.)

This story is based on the folk belief that witches can change shape. In this tale, as in many others, a witch tries to harm a newborn child, but is overcome by those helping with the birth. Usually this role is played by the midwife, but in this story it is the husband who saves his wife and child from the witch. This story demonstrates the loyalty of the husband to his wife and child in fending off the attacks of the witch Barusha. Such loyalty is at the core of Jewish values.

The Sabbath Walking Stick (Turkey)

This story was previously unpublished. (IFA 8896. Collected by David Giddon from Sarah Giddon. AT 560-649, general group.)

The butterfly is a symbol of the soul in Jewish folklore, especially in the Sephardic tradition. It is believed that after a person dies, the soul becomes a butterfly and flies around until it reaches its final place in Heaven.

This story shows the importance of the Sabbath to the Jewish people, and emphasizes the importance of sharing and hospitality, as we see in the biblical story of Abraham.

Amsha the Giant (Iraq)

This story was previously unpublished. (IFA 3615, collected by Yakov Avitsuk from Saayid Porati. AT 327.) It is a variant of "Jack and the Beanstalk" and "Hansel and Gretel" from Grimm's Fairy Tales.

Tales about giants are popular in Jewish folklore. The best-known giant is Og, whom Noah is said to have brought with him on the ark. Amsha is a famous giant in Iraqi folklore. Frightening as he seems to be at first, he ends up being much like the children who imagined him—with giant-sized problems of his own. The enchanted cave found in this tale strongly echoes Jewish tales about enchanted caves that lead directly to the Holy Land.

The King's Secret (Morocco)

This story was published by Zelda Shneursohn in *Edoth* 1:40, October 1945–July 1948. In the Israel Folktale Archives (IFA) there are many variants of this tale from Morocco, Egypt, Bulgaria, Yemen, Afghanistan, Iraq, and Iraqi Kurdistan.

This story, again, emphasizes the importance of keeping a vow, in this case the promise of the barber not to reveal that the king has horns. He merely whispers it in a cave, yet the secret still gets out. The moral to readers is that a promise to keep a secret must really be kept or there can be dangerous consequences. People all over the world tell the story of the barber who had difficulty keeping the secret. Sometimes he tells it to a cave, or a lake, or he buries it in a hole. Only when the story is told by Jews does the barber tell the secret to a wall. This reflects the midrashic saying, "The Wall has ears" (Leviticus Rabbah 32:2), referring to the Western Wall of the Holy Temple in Jerusalem. Jews believe that God's presence is always at the Wall, and that God hears whatever is said there.

The Fisherman and the Silver Fish (Morocco)

This is a story from the Israel Folktale Archives. (IFA 7282, collected by Yifrah Haviv from Aliza Anidjar from Tangiers, Morocco. AT 555.)

This is a version of "The Fisherman and His Wife" from Grimm's Fairy Tales. Here the magic of the fish's speech is attributed to Moses, who saw that the fish was rewarded with speech after it helped a crippled boy cross the Red Sea. In the Jewish version of this tale, we see that the fisherman, spurred by his wife, asks to share the same knowledge as God, and discovers, in this way, that God not only raises a person up, but also brings a person down. Also, in Jewish thought, man may come close to God, but can never become God.

The Weaving that Saved the Prince (Iraq)

This is a story from the Israel Folktale Archives. (IFA 5019, collected by Dov Noy from Yehezkel Danos. AT 888A*.)

This story is based on the folk proverb, "Money may come and money may go, but a profession lasts forever." It emphasizes the Jewish view of the importance of having a profession. It also shows how wit and cleverness can save a person in a dangerous position. Finally, it demonstrates the love and loyalty between parents and children.

A Family of Demons (Eastern Europe)

This story comes from *Tsefunot ve-Aggadot* (Hebrew), edited by Micha Joseph Bin Gorion (Berditchevsky) (Tel Aviv: Am Oved, 1957).

Among the most popular of Jewish superstitions are those concerning demons. Invisible demons were blamed for all sorts of things that would go wrong, from the fire going out to the wine going bad. This particular tale is a good example of a Jewish nursery tale from which even the youngest children learned about demons, though in ways that weren't too frightening. This story also clearly demonstrates the power of the word of God. When the old rabbi reads from the prayer book, he defeats the demons at once.

The Royal Artists and the Clever King (Eastern Europe)

This is a story from *Kochavay Or* (Hebrew) (Jerusalem: 1896).

This is a story of Rabbi Nachman of Bratzlav. The king (a symbol for God) can easily determine the difference between those who make a real effort and those who pretend they have done so. Thus on Yom Kippur God can look into our hearts and see clearly what reward we deserve.

A Coat for the Moon (Eastern Europe)

This story comes from *Sippurim Niflaim* (Hebrew), edited by Samuel Horowitz (Jerusalem: 1935). (AT 298.)

This story, also one of Rabbi Nachman's, is based on the midrashim about the dialogue between God and the moon. This is a light-hearted story, in the spirit of the stories of Chelm.